Becci Murr...

GRANNY DROPPED HER cHOmpers DOWN THE TOILET

ISBN: 978-1-913944-17-9

Published by Llama House Children's Books

Granny dropped her **CHOMPERS** down the toilet.

In they plopped then splashed right out of sight.

Granny dodged the splatter to avoid it,

And then she turned a funny shade of white...

totally toothless

My

CHOMPEROOS

have fallen down the toilet!

They've slid around the bend without a trace.

I'm feeling rather dotty,

'Cause my pegs are in the potty,

Oh, won't someone
get those teeth
back in my face?

He thrust the plunger in with both his hands,

Then pulled a soggy something from the loo...

This
ROLL OF BOTTY WIPES

was down the toilet!

It slid around the bend without a trace.

My tummy's feeling groggy,
'Cause this loo-roll's really soggy,

Oh, won't someone
get those teeth
back in my face?

She pushed it down the toilet with a grin,

And fished a scented object from the bowl...

This

SLIMY BAR OF SOAP

was down the toilet!

It slid around the bend without a trace.

Your mother looked for teethies,
But found something else completely,

Oh, won't someone
get those teeth
back in my face?

Father wore a pair of rubber gloves.

He reached inside and gave a little shove,
Then pulled a yellow item from the can...

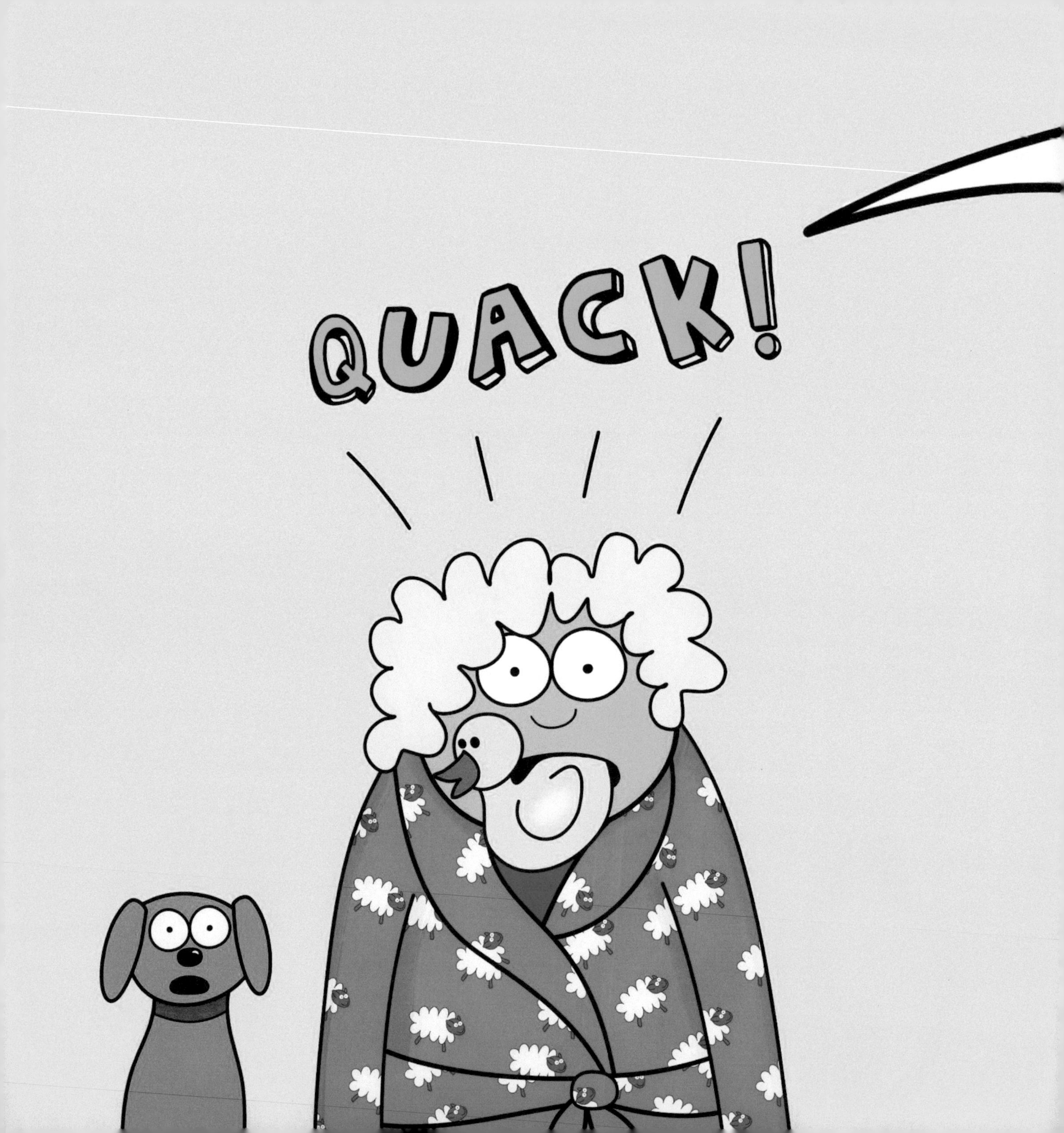
QUACK!

This
SQUEAKY RUBBER DUCK
was down the toilet!

It slid around the bend without a trace.

Your father was unlucky,
To have plucked a rubber ducky,

Oh, won't someone
get those teeth
back in my face?

She swished and fished inside the water trough,
Then raised a set of bristles from the pot...

This
DIRTY SCRUBBING BRUSH
was down the toilet!

It slid around the bend without a trace.

Your auntie went a-fishing,
But my chompers are still missing,

Oh, won't someone
get those teeth
back in my face?

He sunk just like a solid lump of lead,
Then surfaced with a rather tasty snack...

This
YELLOW COB OF CORN
was down the toilet!
It slid around the bend without a trace.

I can't imagine who,
Flushed this sweetcorn down the loo,

Oh, won't someone
get those teeth
back in my face?

Everyone went **POSITIVELY**

"Fear not!" I cried, as Auntie went quite bonkers,

And rushing from the bathroom and the potty...

DOTTY!

quite
bonkers →

smarter
than the
humans
↓

...I SEARCHED THE HOUSE FOR GRAN'S REPLACEMENT CHOMPERS!

WHOOSH!

I snatched a toaster
from the kitchen,

I pulled a painting
from the wall.

WHOOSH!

I searched the garden
for a pigeon,

WHOOSH!

I tried the fish bowl
from the hall.

WHOOSH!

I found a tub and put my hand in,

And grabbed a pair of Uncle's smelly socks,

Then - WHOOSH! - I searched the bedroom and the landing,

And found some dressing-up clothes in a box.

TOY BOX

These

SCARY FANGS

did not fall down the toilet!
And now your grandma's cool beyond belief.

This granny is a beauty,
'Cause these gnashers really suit me,

But...

MORE GRANNY BOOKS...

COLLECT THEM ALL!

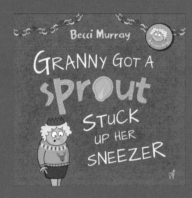

Becci Murray

GRANNY GOT A **sprout** STUCK UP HER SNEEZER

Becci Murray

GRANNY DROPPED HER **chompers** DOWN THE TOILET

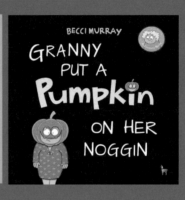

BECCI MURRAY

GRANNY PUT A **Pumpkin** ON HER NOGGIN

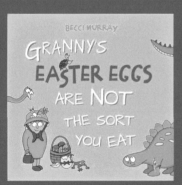

BECCI MURRAY

GRANNY'S EASTER EGGS ARE NOT THE SORT YOU EAT

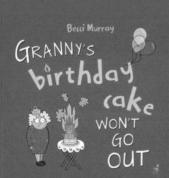

Becci Murray

GRANNY'S **birthday cake** WON'T GO OUT

Becci Murray

GRANDPA'S **CRACKER** WON'T GO BANG

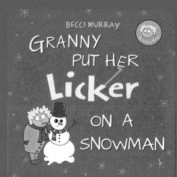

BECCI MURRAY

GRANNY PUT HER **Licker** ON A SNOWMAN

www.llamahousebooks.com

From the author and illustrator of the Granny books...

UNICORN ISLAND

SERIES 1 OUT NOW!

series one stars the unicorns of Munch Town →

Explore the new illustrated chapter book series for ages 4 - 8 years!

Becci Murray
(author)

Becci Murray is a British author from Gloucestershire. She previously wrote for children's television and is the creator of the ever-growing Granny book series.

If you enjoyed Granny Dropped Her Chompers Down the Toilet, please consider leaving a review wherever you purchased the book to help other young readers discover the story.

www.llamahousebooks.com